Stories to ma

For Beginning Readers
Ages 6-8

This series of spooky stories has been created especially for beginning readers—children in first and second grades who are developing their reading skills.

How do these books help children learn to read?

- Kids love creepy stories and these stories are true page-turners (but never too scary).
- The sentences are short.
- The words are simple and repeated often in the story.
- The type is large with lots of room between words and lines.
- Full-color pictures on every page act as visual "clues" to help children figure out the words on the page.

Once children have read one story, they'll be asking for more!

To Laurie, who is just perfect enough—D.H.

For Nicole, who always liked spooky stuff—D.K.R.

Text copyright © 1999 by Deborah Heiligman. Illustrations copyright © 1999 by Deborah
Kogan Ray. All rights reserved. Published by Grosset & Dunlap, Inc., a member of Penguin
Putnam Books for Young Readers, New York. EEK! STORIES TO MAKE YOU SHRIEK
is a trademark of The Putnam & Grosset Group. GROSSET & DUNLAP is a trademark of
Grosset & Dunlap, Inc. Published simultaneously in Canada. Printed in the U.S.A.

Library of Congress Cataloging-in-Publication Data

Heiligman, Deborah.
  Too perfect / by Deborah Heiligman ; illustrated by Deborah Kogan Ray.
    p. cm. — (Eek! Stories to make you shriek)
  Summary: After moving to a town where all the kids are perfect, Sarah makes a
horrifying discovery in the Computer Room of her new school.
  [1. Schools—Fiction. 2. Horror stories.] I. Ray, Deborah Kogan, 1940- ill. II. Title.
III. Series
PZ7.H3673To   1999
[E]—dc21   98-51945
                                                                              CIP
ISBN 0-448-41960-2   A B C D E F G H I J   AC

Too Perfect

By Deborah Heiligman

Illustrated by Deborah Kogan Ray

Grosset & Dunlap • New York

I do not want to move.

I like my house.

I like my school.

And my friends.

But Mom says I will love our new town.

It's called Blissville.

"It's perfect," she says.

Our new house is pretty cool.

It has a great big yard.

And I see a lot of kids on our block.

Two girls are jumping rope.

They are so good at it.

They never mess up.

Down the street,

two boys are shooting hoops.

Wow! They make every basket.

They don't push each other.

They don't fight.

It's so nice out, too.

Birds are singing.

All the flowers are in bloom.

It's just like a movie!

I run back into our new house.

"Mom, this town is perfect!"
I say.

"I told you so," she says.

And then she frowns.

"Oh, Sarah. Look what you did!"

Uh-oh. I've gotten mud

all over the floor.

As usual.

"Sorry," I say.

"Nobody's perfect."

It's my first day of school.

Mom got me a new dress.

But I put on my old jeans.

"How can you wear

those sloppy jeans today?"

Mom scolds.

"They're my good luck pair,"

I tell her.

"And I need them today."

I'm nervous.

Kids are always mean to the new kid.

They make fun of you.

They leave you out.

I don't want to be the new kid!

I walk to school all alone.

In the classroom, my new teacher says,

"Boys and girls, say hello to Sarah."

"Hello, Sarah," they say.

They all smile. Great big smiles.

"You may sit next to Brian,"

says the teacher.

"He's new, too. He started last week."

Brian makes a funny face at me.

I giggle.

"This place is weird," he whispers.

The teacher shoots Brian a look.

"No talking in class," she says.

"Yes, your majesty," he says.

No one laughs. Except for me.

The teacher leans on Brian's desk.

"Brian, do you like computers?" she asks.

"Sure," he says.

"Good," she says.

"Soon it will be time for you

to go to the Computer Room."

At lunch, I sit with Brian
and a girl named Wendy.
Wendy is pretty boring.
All she says are things like,
"The spelling test was fun."
"Isn't it a lovely day?"
"This liver is so yummy."
Is she for real?

At recess we play soccer.

Nobody fights.

Nobody falls.

Nobody fouls—except for Brian.

Nobody gets dirty—except for me.

Each team scores five goals.

"Oh goody," one boy says.

"A tie! When we tie, everyone wins!"

I roll my eyes at Brian.

"See what I mean?" he says.

"This place is really weird."

After recess, the teacher says,

"It's quiet time.

Everybody will be quiet for an hour."

An hour?

How can we be quiet for a whole hour?

I look over at Brian.

"Bor-ing," he whispers.

Everybody else just nods happily.

Then they sit still and stare into space.

I can't stand it.

After ten minutes, I poke Brian.

"I can't believe she's making us sit here."

Brian laughs.

"This teacher is a dork!"

he says in a loud voice.

The teacher looks up from her book.

"Brian, are you talking during quiet time?"

"Yes," Brian says.

"That's it," the teacher says.

"It's time for you to go to the Computer

Room."

"I was talking, too," I say.

"Can I go with him?"

The teacher smiles. "Don't worry, Sarah.

Your turn will come."

After a long time, Brian comes back.

I make my fish face

and wait for him to laugh.

But he just sits in his seat.

He doesn't say anything to me.

"So how was it?" I whisper.

"Do they have cool computers?"

Brian turns to me.

He looks different.

His eyes seem kind of empty.

"No talking in class," he says.

"Very funny," I say.

"Teacher," says Brian.

"Sarah is talking in class."

I stare at Brian.

What is going on?

I don't know.

But this place is starting

to give me the creeps.

As soon as school is over, I run home.

I grab a snack and plop down.

Mom walks in the door.

"How was school today?" she asks.

"Creepy," I say. "Mom, can we move?"

She does not say yes or no.

She says, "Sarah, look at this mess!"

Oops! I got some pizza on the sofa.

"Sorry. I'll clean it up later," I say.

"But Mom, listen.

The kids here are weird.

They're too nice, too polite,

and too quiet."

"Are they clean and neat?" Mom asks.

"Yeah! Nobody ever gets dirty!" I say.

"They're all perfect."

Mom smiles.

"How lovely," she says.

"Now clean up the pizza!"

I didn't want to come back
to school today.
But, of course, I had to.
Everything is perfect again.

Perfect homework papers.

Perfect smiles.

Perfect children.

All perfect except me.

When it's quiet time, I groan.

"Not again!"

"Sarah," says the teacher.

"We must get you to

the Computer Room soon.

I'll try to get you in tomorrow."

There is something in her voice

I don't like.

Why is she in such a rush

to get me there?

I raise my hand.

I ask to go to the bathroom.

I can not stand any more quiet time.

I am going to check out

the Computer Room.

What luck!

Some kids are walking there right now.

I step into line and go in with them.

Then I hide behind a desk.

This sure doesn't look like

the Computer Room at my old school.

There are people in white coats.

They are putting wires on each kid's head.

The wires come from one large computer.

"What are we
working on today?"
one white coat asks.
"Manners and chores,"
says another white coat.
"Each child will do
three hours of chores every day.
And now each child
will always say 'Please'
and 'Thank you.'"

The first white coat

hits a big red button.

A loud buzzer goes off.

"Thank you for letting us

do more chores,"

the kids say all together.

"Please let us

go back to class now."

I put my hand over my mouth

so I won't scream.

That's why all

the kids seem perfect.

They are wired to be perfect!

I have to get out of here fast!

Before they mess with my brain!

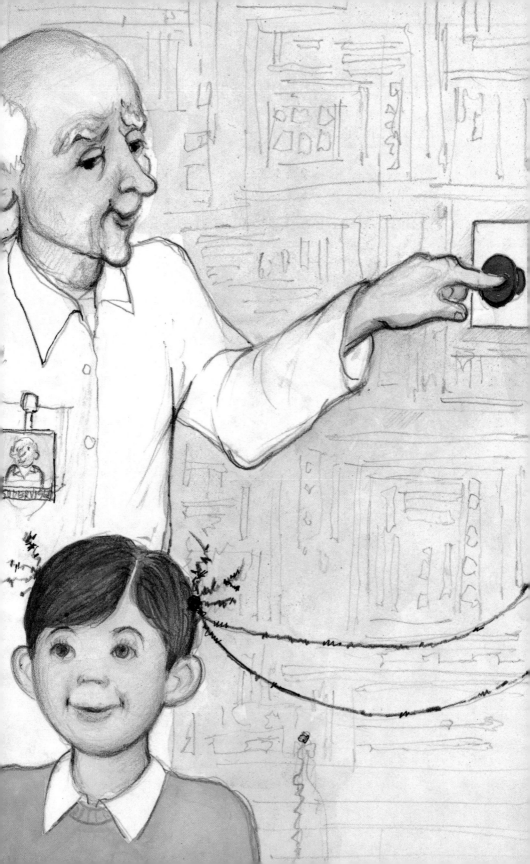

I jump up and pull open the door.

An alarm goes off.

Lights flash.

"Stop that girl!" someone yells.

I run down the hall as fast as I can.

But just as I reach the door,

someone grabs my arm.

It's my teacher!

"Not so fast, Sarah," she says.

Two white coats take me back to

the Computer Room.

"Help!" I yell.

"I don't want to be perfect!"

"This will only take a moment,"

a white coat tells me.

"And it won't hurt a bit."

It is so nice out today.

The birds are singing.

All the flowers are in bloom.

I wipe my shoes on the mat.

Then I take them off

and put them neatly by the door.

"Hi, Mom," I say. "I'm home."

"How was school today?" she asks.

"Perfect," I say.